DRAW
A PERFECT PRINCESS
1
2
3
4
5
6

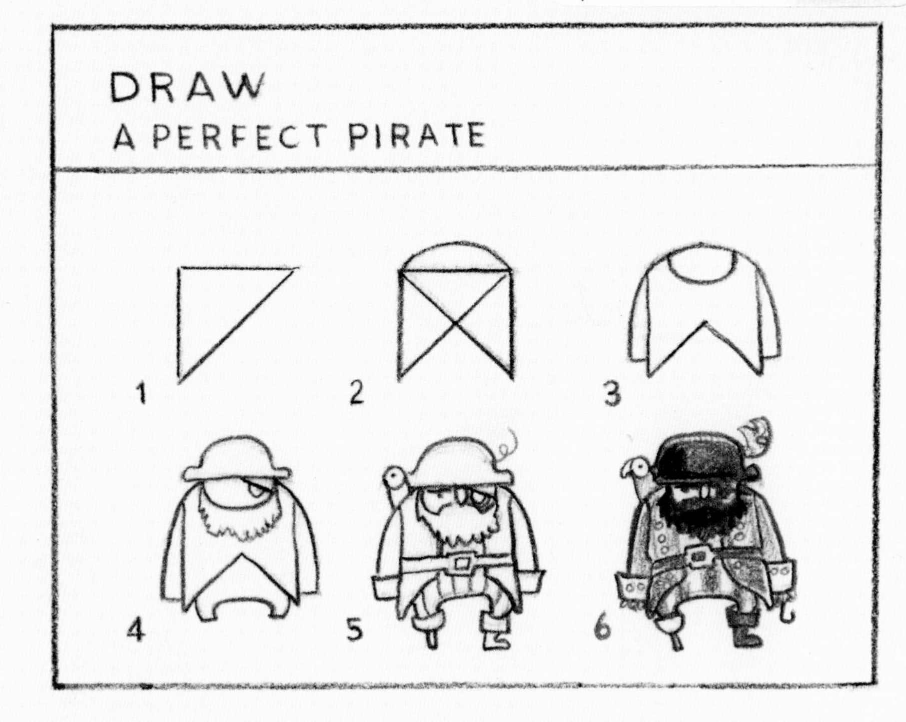
DRAW
A PERFECT PIRATE
1
2
3
4
5
6

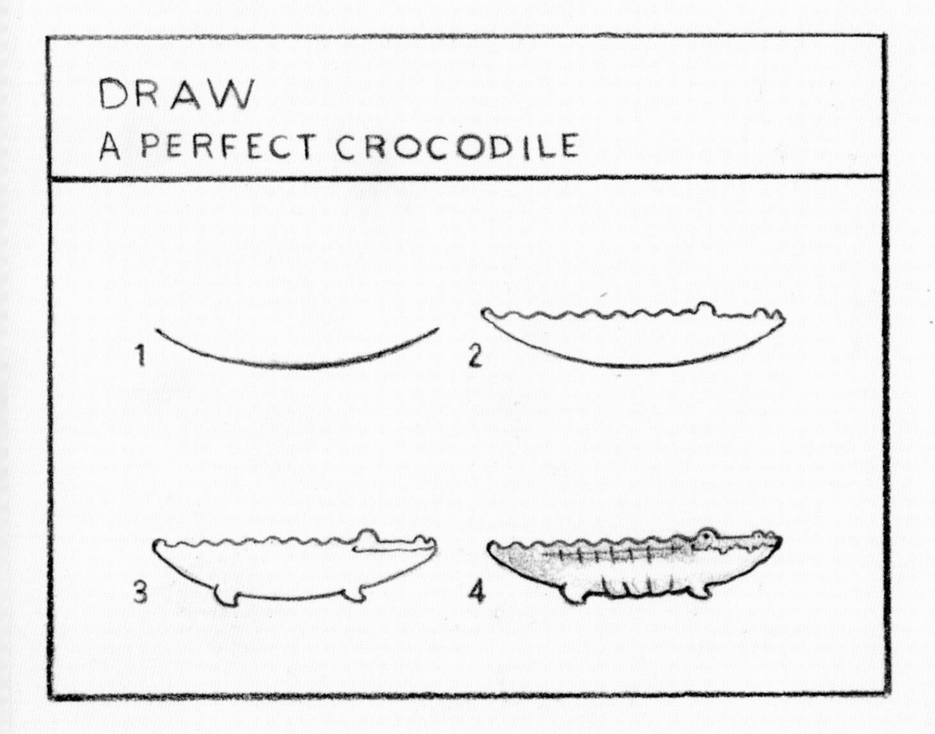
DRAW
A PERFECT CROCODILE
1
2
3
4

DRAW
SOMETHING PERFECT

*For my Alex*

SIMON & SCHUSTER BOOKS FOR YOUNG READERS
An imprint of Simon & Schuster Children's Publishing Division
1230 Avenue of the Americas, New York, New York 10020

For information about special discounts for bulk purchases, please contact Simon & Schuster Special Sales
at 1-866-506-1949 or business@simonandschuster.com.
The Simon & Schuster Speakers Bureau can bring authors to your live event. For more information
or to book an event, contact the Simon & Schuster Speakers Bureau at 1-866-248-3049
or visit our website at www.simonspeakers.com.
Book design by Laurent Linn
The text for this book was set in Plumbsky.
The illustrations for this book were rendered in watercolor, gouache, pastel,
and colored pencil on watercolor paper.
Manufactured in China
0620 SCP
First Edition
2 4 6 8 10 9 7 5 3 1
Library of Congress Cataloging-in-Publication Data
Names: Bates, Amy June, author, illustrator.
Title: When I draw a panda / Amy June Bates.
Description: First edition. | New York : Simon & Schuster Books for Young Readers, Paula Wiseman Books, [2020] |
Audience: Ages 4-8. | Audience: Grades 2-3. | Summary: "A girl draws an unusual panda, who comes to life and draws all
sorts of whimsical things with her, from a castle to a dragon and more"— Provided by publisher.
Identifiers: LCCN 2019052818 (print) | LCCN 2019052819 (eBook) |
ISBN 9781481451482 (hardback) | ISBN 9781481451499 (eBook)
Subjects: CYAC: Drawing—Fiction. | Individuality—Fiction. | Imagination—Fiction. | Pandas—Fiction.
Classification: LCC PZ7.B2944446 Whe 2020 (print) | LCC PZ7.B2944446 (eBook) | DDC [E]—dc23
LC record available at https://lccn.loc.gov/2019052818
LC ebook record available at https://lccn.loc.gov/2019052819

# When I Draw a Panda

AMY JUNE BATES

A Paula Wiseman Book
SIMON & SCHUSTER BOOKS FOR YOUNG READERS
New York London Toronto Sydney New Delhi

Sometimes when they say
to draw a perfect circle,
mine turns out a little wonky.

I can draw a perfect fluffy cloud,
a perfect scoop of ice cream,
and a perfect flat tire.

So when I draw a panda,

I keep drawing more and more
not-perfect circles until I see a panda.

Then I step back and think,
*What* **else** *does a panda need?*

He probably needs a hat,
and then he is **my** panda.

My panda draws his own way.

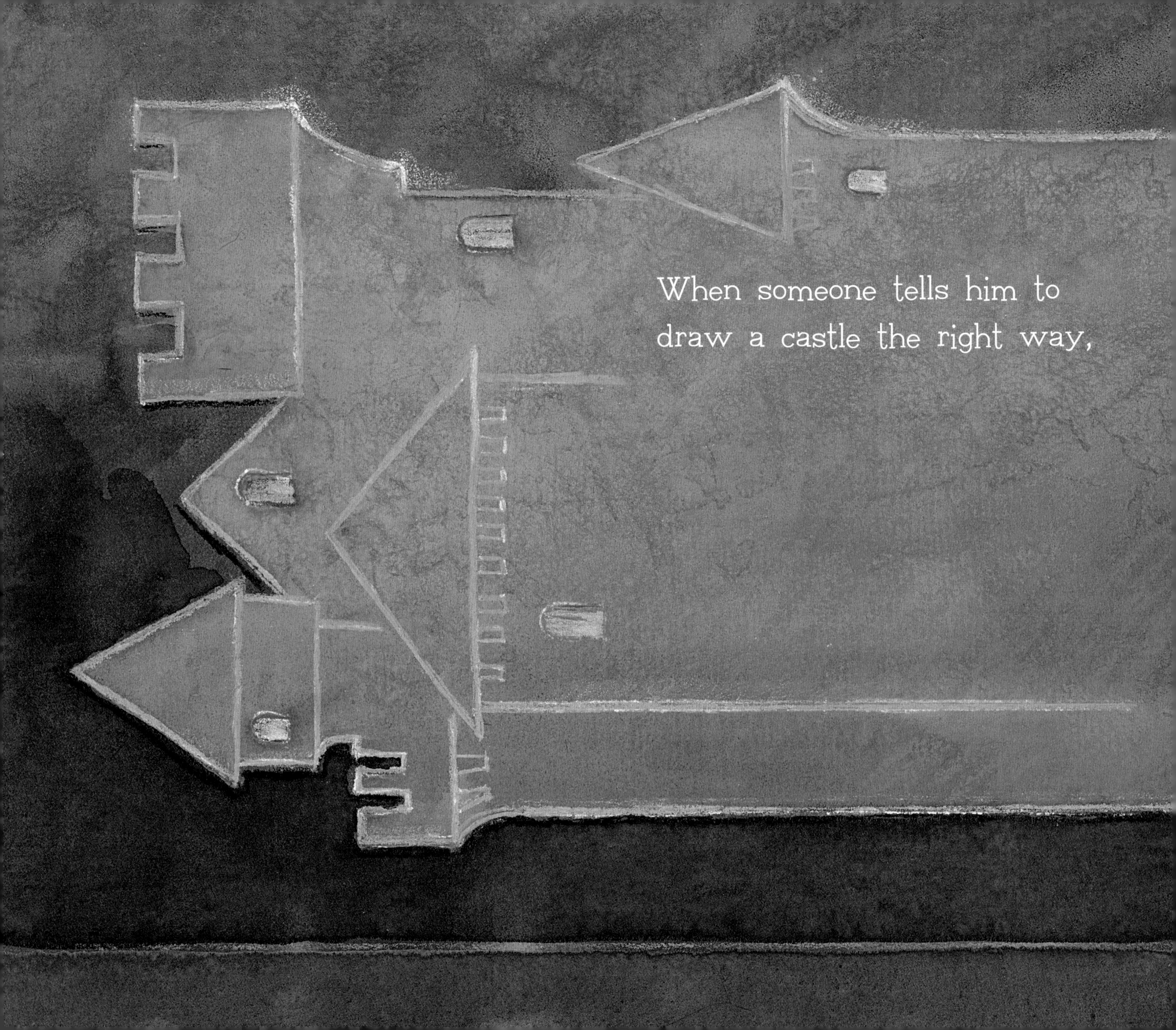

When someone tells him to
draw a castle the right way,

he would rather draw it the left way.

And if they tell him to draw something pretty,

he draws something pretty silly.

My panda shows me how
to draw a **dragon**:

1. Draw a squiggle.

2. Decide which end is the head and which is the tail.

3. Draw the tail last.

Sometimes when they say to draw
a perfect pirate, superhero, crocodile,
mad scientist, or princess,

my panda prefers to draw an imperfect,

super heroic,

madly scientific,

piratical princess

crocodile.

Sometimes when they say to draw
a perfect bowl of fruit,
my panda looks out the window

and watches a butterfly.

Then he thinks about what it
would be like to **be** a butterfly

until he has totally forgotten

what he was

supposed

to be

drawing.

I can draw my own way too.

Sometimes when they saw to draw it "this way,"
I ask, "Why?"

And when they say, "Draw it that way,"
I do,

but I add a **unicorn horn** later.

Sometimes they say, "That will never work."

But it does.

Sometimes they say, "Make sure you don't run out of space."

But I didn't, so I do.

Sometimes they can't figure out what we have drawn and then it is a **mystery**, because we will **never** tell them.

Sometimes they say, "You and your panda draw **too crazy**," and I say,

"Thank you."

Sometimes we are supposed
to draw quietly.

But we can't help it.
Our pencils like to ROAR!

Sometimes lines come out of our
pencils and they are not going

anywhere

in

particular.

They are just going somewhere
that makes us happy.

DRAW
A PERFECT CIRCLE

DRAW
A PERFECT PANDA

DRAW
A PERFECT DRAGON

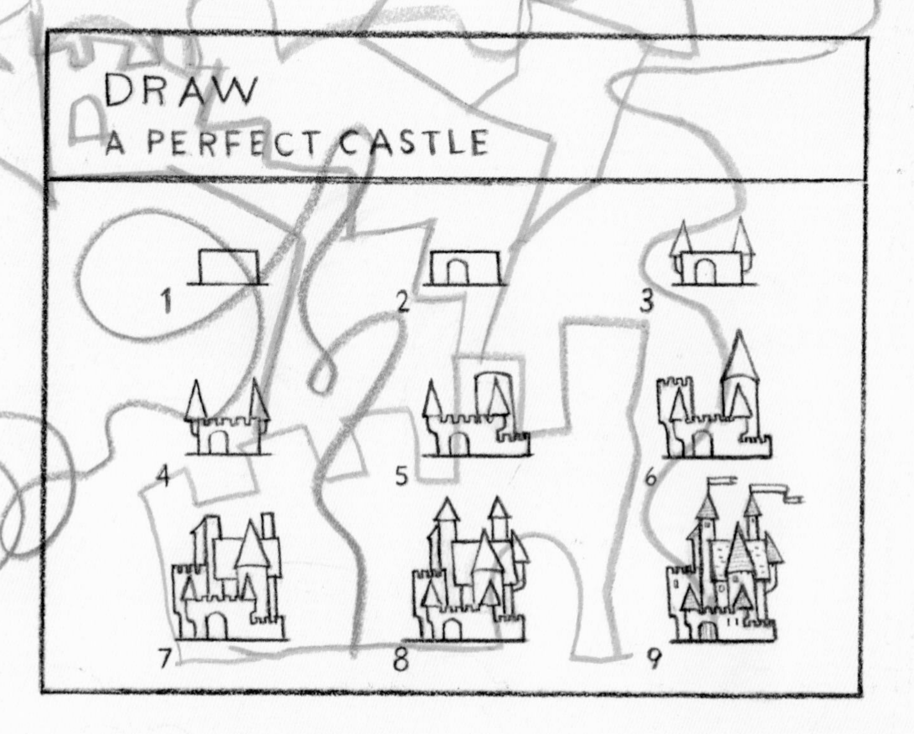
DRAW
A PERFECT CASTLE